For Milo, with love

First published in Great Britain by HarperCollins Children's Books Ltd in 2007

1 3 5 7 9 10 8 6 4 2

ISBN-13: 978-0-00-720785-5
ISBN-10: 0-00-720785-9

HarperCollins Children's Books is a division of HarperCollins Publishers Ltd.
Text and illustrations copyright © Jan Fearnley 2007

The author/illustrator asserts the moral right to be identified as the author/illustrator of the work.
A CIP catalogue record for this title is available from the British Library. All rights reserved.
No part of this publication may be reproduced, stored in a retrieval system or transmitted in any
form or by any means, electronic, mechanical, photocopying, recording or otherwise, without the
prior permission of HarperCollins Publishers Ltd, 77-85 Fulham Palace Road,
Hammersmith, London W6 8JB.

Visit our website at: harpercollinschildrensbooks.co.uk

Printed and bound by Printing Express, Hong Kong

Are We There Yet?*

Jan Fearnley

The infamous purple blanket!

Dad complaining about everyone else's driving. He says he's the best driver ever.

Travel Sweets

HarperCollins *Children's Books*

It was a lovely sunny day. The Tibbles family were going to see Gran and Grandad. Mum, Dad, Twinkle, Billy and Little Eric all helped to pack the car.

Billy sorted out
everything he
needed.

Little Eric, the baby,
sat on his purple
blanket, playing with
the daisies.

Dad was bossing everyone around.

"Hurry up!" he said. "We mustn't be late."

"My blanket," said Little Eric.

They all climbed in and off they went...

Vrrooo0Oo0OooOom*!

"Don't drive so fast," said Mum.

"Are we there yet?" said Billy.

"I feel sick," said Twinkle.

"Don't hassle me while I'm driving!" yelled Dad.

"I want my blanket," thought Little Eric.

Vroo00ooOM! On they went.

They hadn't gone far when...

"Dad," said Twinkle, "I've forgotten my trumpet."

"Do you really need it?" sighed Dad.

"Oh yes, I really do. I promised Grandad I'd play
him my new tune," said Twinkle.

Grumpily, Dad turned the car around. They went back up the road, back home again.

Twinkle fetched her trumpet.

"Now I can serenade you all the way," she said, skipping to the car.

"Terrific," said Dad.

"My blanket!" said Little Eric.

Off they went again, in the lovely sunshine. vrooOOOOOOooOOM!*

Down the road and round the corner. Then…

"Mum, I need the toilet," said Billy.

"Oh," said Mum. "Are you sure?"

"Yes. I need it NOW!"

Dad turned the
car around.
*Back round
the corner...
back down the road...
all the way back home.*
"You should have gone
before we set out,"
grumbled Dad.
"I forgot," said Billy.
"There's my blanket!"
said Little Eric.

Off they went again...
down the road...
round the corner...
past the park.
"Are we there yet?"
asked Billy.
Then...

"Oh!" said Mum.
"I forgot to close
the window."
"Not you as well,"
moaned Dad.

Back past the park...
round the corner...
down the road...
and all the way home.

"It was locked all the time!" Mum laughed.

"Great," said Dad, not laughing.

"Now can we go?"

Vrooooooooooooooooooo OM!

*Off they went...
down the road...
round the corner...
past the park...
over the bridge...*

"Did I lock the front door?" asked Mum.
"YES!" said Dad. "Must I be the one who always remembers everything?"

Vrooooooooooooooooooo OM!

went the car,
through the town...

Twinkle practised on her trumpet:

Tootle-ootle, ootle-ootle, ooootle!

Billy had a go on his bubble blaster:

Bubbubbubbubbubb!

The car sped past the fountain:

VroOooOOOOOM!

MeeeeEeeeoWw

went the children, and
they began to fight.
Slappity slap!
Nippety nip!
Pinchety pinch!
"QUIET!"
yelled Dad.
"You'll wake
up the baby."

SLAP!

PINch!

"OH, NO! THE BABY!"

"WHERE IS
THE BABY?"

So quickly they went…

vrooOooOM

back past the fountain…

vrooOooOM

back through the town…

Chocolaterie

DENTIST

Fruity Tutti

vrooOooOM

over the bridge…

vrOOOoOM

past the park...

vrOOOoOM

round the corner...

vrOOOoOM

Screech!

round the van too...

Mister Banana

vrOOOoOM

*back down
the road...
and all the
way home.*

Phew!

There was Little Eric, sitting on his purple blanket, playing with the daisies.

"Right," said Dad. "Let's be absolutely sure... Does anybody need the toilet?"

"NO!"

"Is the house locked up?"

"YES!"

"Have we remembered everything?"

"YES!"

"Including the baby?"

"YES!"

"Okay," said Dad.

"LET'S GO!"

Off they went...
down the road, round the corner,
past the park, over the bridge,
through the town, past the fountain...

Then...

phut, phut, phut, went the car and it stopped.
"What's the matter now?" asked Mum.

"I don't believe it,"
said Dad. "I forgot to
get some petrol."

Dad's forgotten the petrol !*
Dad's forgotten the petrol !*

It wasn't far to Gran and Grandad's house,
so they walked the rest of the way.

"Are we there yet?"
asked Billy.

They were very late
when Gran answered the
door. "Ooh," she said,
"How lovely!" She'd
completely forgotten
they were coming!

It didn't matter.
They all remembered
the most important thing –
to have a lovely time together.

And everyone agreed it had certainly
been a journey they would never forget.

And much, much later,

Dad and Billy went to fetch the car.

They were gone for a very long time,

because Dad had forgotten where he'd left it.